Author's Note

The practice of yoga naturally lends itself to children because many yoga poses imitate things we find in nature. Children love to pretend they are trees or animals, and as they imitate the natural world around them, they connect with it and appreciate it on a deeper level.

Yoga is normally practiced barefoot for better balance and grip. (A sticky mat is useful but not essential.) Yoga is not about competition. Listen to your body. Never push yourself or force the postures. Keep your body relaxed and your breath slow and steady.

Namaste (Na-mah-stay). (The spirit in me honors the spirit in you.)

—Kathy Beliveau

For my sisters, Suzanne, Dianne and Colette. How lucky were
we to grow up by the sea! And as always, for my own amazing
family. With oceans of love. -K.B.

For my mom, who let me take art classes instead of math. -D.H.

Published in 2014 by Simply Read Books www.simplyreadbooks.com

Text © 2014 Kathy Beliveau. Illustrations © 2014 Denise Holmes

Library and Archives Canada Cataloguing in Publication

Beliveau, Kathy, 1962-, author
The yoga game by the sea / written by Kathy Beliveau
; illustrated by Denise Holmes.
ISBN 978-1-927018-49-1 (bound)
1. Hatha yoga--Juvenile literature. I. Holmes, Denise,
illustrator II. Title.

RA781.7.B452 2014   j613.7'046   C2014-900441-9

We gratefully acknowledge for their financial support of our publishing program the Canada Council for the Arts, the BC Arts Council, and the
Government of Canada through the Canada Book Fund (CBF).

Manufactured in Malaysia. Book design by Sara Gillingham Studio.

10 9 8 7 6 5 4 3 2 1

THE YOGA GAME

BY THE SEA

by Kathy Beliveau • illustrated by Denise Holmes

SIMPLY READ BOOKS

Wiggle your toes and touch your nose.
Now can you guess the yoga pose?
First we listen to the clue,
then we see what we can do!

fig. 1

fig. 2

I wrap the world in seven seas.
Pirates sail on my breeze.
My tides are low. My tides are high.
Each wave is like a breath and sigh.

What am I?

Sleek and graceful in the sea,
on land I flop more awkwardly.
Smooth and round with flippered feet.
Think of all the fish I eat.

What am I?

I am a **seal!**

I burst up through the warm blue sea,
then dive down low and splash with glee.
I click and cluck and whistle sound.
My laughter bubbles all around.

What am I?

I can reach way up high
and paint my magic in the sky.
Radiant colors everywhere.
See them balance in the air.

What am I?

I am a **rainbow!**

Come and sing a lullaby
to the crescent in the sky.
Sometimes I am full and bright,
a brilliant glowing ball of light!

What am I?

I am the moon!

I soar above the land and sea
or sit upon a giant tree.
Perching poised with piercing eyes,
I silently search sea and skies.

What am I?

People row or paddle me.
I can sail across the sea,
with a captain and a crew,
to navigate the endless blue.

What am I?

To get across from A to B,
you might go up and over me,
or sail under in a boat
or sneak across a castle's moat.

What am I?

I am a **bridge!**

Would you like to live with me. . .
swimming in the deep blue sea?
Glistening fins and shiny scales,
hanging out with clams and whales?

What am I?

A squishy blob inside my shell,
this round hinged home is where I dwell.
I try to burrow in the sands
to hide from gulls and digging hands.

What am I?

I am a clam!

I breathe the air, the air breathes me.
I am the land. I am the sea.
I am the clouds that drift above.
I am special. I am love.

what am I?

I am **me!**

Namaste.